The Rainy Day Grump

By Deborah Eaton
Photographs by Dorothy Handelman

M
The Millbrook Press
Brookfield, Connecticut

It was raining, and that was bad news.
On rainy days
Clay was always a grump.
You cannot play ball in the rain.
And Clay LOVED to play ball.

"Come on, Clay," said his sister, Rosie.
"Come play with me."
But Clay just sat there.

Rosie made a sign.
NO GRUMPS!
She marched up and down.
Clay looked out the window.

"I know," said Rosie.
"We can play dress-up."
She pulled this and that
out of a big, old box.
Soon she was a pirate.
"YO-HO-HO!" she yelled.

Clay put his hands over his ears.
"Forget it!" he said.
But Rosie pulled him onto her ship
and set sail for far-off lands.
On the way they passed a whale.

The Rainy Day Grump
tossed his ball up and down.
He did not want to play this game.
"Go walk the plank," he told Rosie.
"What a grump!" said Rosie.
But she did it, just for fun.
"Glug, glug, glug."

13

Rosie put on a white hat and a star.
"I'll be the good guy," she told Clay.
"You can be the bad guy."

She put a black hat on his head.
Then she gave him a horse to ride.

Rosie rode her horse fast.
She roped nine or ten bad guys.
Then she roped herself.

Clay laughed and laughed.

Rosie made a face.
She patted her tin star.
"You better be good, Clay," she said.
"If you're not,
I'll have to put you in jail."

The Rainy Day Grump
hit some home runs.
"Give up, Rosie," he said.
"I want to play ball, not dress-up."

But she did not give up.
Not Rosie.
"What about this?" she asked.

Clay had to grin.
"Put it on," said Rosie.
"You can be king of the clowns.
I will be the queen bee."

She tried to sting Clay.
But he was too fast for her.

"You need more clown stuff,"
said Rosie.
She looked in the box.
"How about this?
Do you want to go for a swim?"

27

"No way!" said Clay.
"But I know what we can play next."
He told Rosie his plan.
"No more Rainy Day Grump!"
said Rosie.
"This will be the best dress-up yet."

It was still raining.
But Clay and Rosie did not care.
You can get as wet as you want
in a swimsuit.
"Let's go, Rosie!" said Clay.
"Let's play ball."

A Note to Parents

Welcome to REAL KIDS READERS, a series of phonics-based books for children who are beginning to read. In the classroom, educators use phonics to teach children how to sound out unfamiliar words, providing a firm foundation for reading skills. At home, you can use REAL KIDS READERS to reinforce and build on that foundation, because the books follow the same basic phonic guidelines that children learn in school.

Of course the best way to help your child become a good reader is to make the experience fun—and REAL KIDS READERS do that, too. With their realistic story lines and lively characters, the books engage children's imaginations. With their clean design and sparkling photographs, they provide picture clues that help new readers decipher the text. The combination is sure to entertain young children and make them truly want to read.

REAL KIDS READERS have been developed at three distinct levels to make it easy for children to read at their own pace.

- LEVEL 1 is for children who are just beginning to read.
- LEVEL 2 is for children who can read with help.
- LEVEL 3 is for children who can read on their own.

A controlled vocabulary provides the framework at each level. Repetition, rhyme, and humor help increase word skills. Because children can understand the words and follow the stories, they quickly develop confidence. They go back to each book again and again, increasing their proficiency and sense of accomplishment, until they're ready to move on to the next level. The result is a rich and rewarding experience that will help them develop a lifelong love of reading.

For Jackson and, of course, for Clay
—D.E.

Special thanks to Hanna Andersson, Portland, OR, and to Cricket Hosiery for providing clothing; to East End Sporting Goods, Mattituck, NY, for providing sports equipment; to FAO Schwarz for providing toys and costumes; to Little Eric Shoes, NYC, for providing shoes; to Jon Bressler & Co.; and to Mary Ellen Carlson, a.k.a. the Grandma Boutique.

Produced by DWAI / Seventeenth Street Productions, Inc.
Reading Specialist: Virginia Grant Clammer

Library of Congress Cataloging-in-Publication Data
Eaton, Deborah.
   The rainy day grump / Deborah Eaton ; photographs by Dorothy Handelman.
        p.   cm. — (Real kids readers. Level 2)
   Summary: Rosie wants her brother Clay to play dress-up, but he is grumpy because it's raining and they can't play ball.
   ISBN 0-7613-2018-0 (lib. bdg.). — ISBN 0-7613-2043-1 (pbk.)
   [1. Rain and rainfall—Fiction. 2. Baseball—Fiction. 3. Play—Fiction. 4. Brothers and sisters—Fiction.] I. Handelman, Dorothy, ill. II. Title. III. Series.
PZ7.E1338Ra1 1998
[E]—dc21   98-10044
                                                                                         CIP
                                                                                         AC

pbk: 10 9 8 7 6 5 4 3 2 1
lib: 10 9 8 7 6 5 4 3 2 1